# To Become a Flower

# A Book By CEON

Printed and bound in Great Britain by:
Book Printing UK Remus House, Coltsfoot Drive,
Woodston, Peterborough, PE2 9BF

ISBN: 978-1-3999-9061-5

CEON is a queer Scottish author. Their first novel 'The Condition: Impervious' was published March 2022, in the Thriller genre at 23 years old. Their second book 'Allure' came out November 2023 (Urban Fantasy / Dark Romance). They have also been published in various magazines / zines for poetry and life stories. They aim for all of their books to have queer and mental health representation.

# Acknowledgements

Thank you to Poppy and Kittie for being the cutest fluffy family members (yes, I am giving thanks to my cats).

Special thanks to Elinor Prescott for lending her artistic skills for the cover typeface and to Evangeline Gallagher for her fantastic cover art.

# Acknowledgements

# Chapter One

There are a lot of shadow people here, in these woods. Those are not words I'd ever speak aloud, because of my mum. Now all eyes are always on me, but only from the side, folk wouldn't dare to look at me straight on. So I'm not allowed to say things that may even in the slightest be seen as weird, which means I don't talk often. Everyone is so judgemental about everything, because their way of life is the only way of life.

Walking through the trees in the pitch-black, watching the peering eyes, but trying not to let them know that I'd noticed their existence, when a movement in the corner of my eye caught my attention. A man approached saying something I couldn't hear. I felt a sting in my chest, causing a bolt to flash through my body, running through down my right leg, seemingly affecting my whole body. He was still talking while approaching, there was no way to ignore him. I took my headphone out.

"Ye got a light?"

I shook my head, frozen in place. When he got closer and saw my face he took a step back, quickly shuffling away from me when he realised who I was. Gundichley is a small place - so everyone knows each other, therefore everyone knows to avoid me.

Why would a young woman, who is always on edge, be walking through the woods at 1am? Well, it's the only way I could get to work from my house. Because of the incident, most jobs were scared to take me on as a worker but the townspeople had no problem tucking me away in the antisocial hours of a factory job, beside all the other people (men) who couldn't get jobs, or had harsh backgrounds. Still, with the low level of people I worked with: I was the worst. Maybe they were scared of me too, or maybe it was sexism, I wouldn't know - but none of my co-workers spoke to me, not when anyone else was around that is.

This morning we had a meeting, something about working harder, reaching our numbers. I wasn't really listening. I never worked hard, and I never got pulled up for it because my bosses were too scared. Honestly; I didn't even need a job, but it was just something to do. From across the room I saw Abel looking around, making sure no one was looking in his direction, before looking up at me, nodding and quickly looking at the bosses too, pretending he was listening. I knew what that nod meant. It was to say: 'I'll be seeing you tonight'.

# Chapter Two

The incident happened when I was sixteen. They knew no one would take me; so instead of putting me into the care system they let me stay at home and gave me some money to get along. Even though it was a few years ago, no one will forget. Nothing much happens here anyway, and that incident had seemingly put our town on the map.

I was only a kid when it happened, so my name was never mentioned in reports, and although they changed my second name; Gundichley was so small that everyone knew who I was anyway.

# Chapter Three

Abel was different from the rest of the men we worked with. He was young, for one. He hadn't been in jail, and wasn't the kind of person that struck any sort of fear into anyone. He was probably the closest thing to an 'attractive' man that Gundichley would see.

I lay there, still as a plank as he fired himself into me, grunting, groaning and calling me all sorts of names. He liked degrading, and he only liked me because I'm messed up. This was our routine; he'd tell me he was coming. I'd let him into my home and we'd have sex, then he'd return to his fiancée.

If I was a little more stupid, I'd think this was love; if anything my mum had ever said rubbed off on me it would've sent the message that love means to hate. Having sex with him made me think of her, relive the memories I still had. I didn't stop him, I never said no, I wasn't attracted to him and I wasn't aroused by the thought of sex, but it was something to fill time. Anyway, as I said, if I showed the slightest bit of emotion, I'd be compared to my mum, and they were just begging for a reason to lock me up. Even for as little as speaking my mind. I guess at the very least, I was still wanted by someone, despite everything.

He started getting dressed beside me.

"Do you ever think there's more?"

His head snapped toward me, the mere fact that I had spoken made him visibly tense. I was just a body to him, so the fact that I broke my guarded silence must have frightened him. "More than Gundichley?" I added.

He took a deep breath in and spoke through his exhale, "Not for people like you." and with that he got up and left.

# Chapter Four

I think about the incident often and honestly feel that I may still be living in it, which is strange seeing as I don't remember it. I know I was there, not because people had told me, but because I could still *feel* it, when I tried to remember; there is no sound, no visuals, just a loud feeling. An air that always surrounded me.

I know what happened, I've read about it, and a therapist once tried to explain it to me, but I don't know that day, nor the child I once was, not anymore.

# Chapter Four

# Chapter Five

I had become bored. I don't remember ever being not bored. Last night was the first time I had questioned it out loud, of course to the only person that would object to me leaving Gundichley. Not that I cared about his opinion, but I couldn't help but wonder if my asking him was an attempt to shoot myself in the foot, to shut down the idea of there ever being more for me.

I don't think it was me; but more of what was left of my mother inside of me, trying to sabotage me. So today I looked online and found a flat for sale in West Roimhik. I called the estate agency and made an offer. They were very insistent of me going for a viewing, but eventually after me persisting; they sold it to me. I still had most of the money I was given as a teen, plus what I earned at the factory. I owned our family home, paying off the mortgage is probably the only good thing my parents had done for me, and they didn't even do it for me. Nothing happened here in Gundichley so I never paid for outings or hobbies. I just worked and fucked Abel, well, more realistically lay there while he fucked me.

That morning at work he nodded at me again, but this time in response I shook my head which made something unfamiliar flicker in his eyes.

On my way to walk back home, a hand grabbed me from among the trees.

"What do you mean *no*? That's not how this works," Abel sighed and let go of me. "Look at what you're making me risk, out in daylight." He threw his arms around. "Is it because of what you asked last night?"

I pulled him in and kissed him, something we had never done before. Something I had never done with anyone. He was frozen in his surprise, and I took that opportunity to walk away.

I meant more to him than he to me, so I figured he needed that kiss and I was thankful that he gave me something to occupy my time here, as unattached to it as I was.

Now he could try to be an honest man, and stay loyal to the woman that was to become his wife.

# Chapter Six

My father always loved opera music, whenever I heard it I held my breath. I held my breath when they were singing the long notes, to see how much they were risking to sing. When I was small I could never keep up, giving up and gasping for air, once or twice passing out from holding on too long.

Whenever I heard it; I felt scared. Whenever Mother had been especially bad, worse than usual, my Father would put opera on loud and cook me and my brothers dinner when she spent a night away. He'd usually cook my favourite meal, as it was only ever me that she was mean to. It struck fear into me, because every time she returned; she'd be more nasty, extra passive aggressiveness sneaking out at every given opportunity. It scared me because I knew it hurt him, knowing that she hurt me. But empathy doesn't make him a saint, if he didn't do anything about it, it makes him the opposite, actually. To see a wrong and stand by it, letting it happen with no repercussions.

# Chapter Seven

I went home and started filling a backpack with clothes and my toothbrush. Nothing really had any meaning to me, so I only packed essentials.

I locked the door for what I thought would be the last time, until I remembered what I had forgotten. I unlocked the door and sprinted up the stairs, grabbing a sock from under my pillow. Abel's sock, he had once left after one of our many nights together. Then I found a box of pins in one of the kitchen draws. I looked around and breathed in the space. Not for sentimental reasons, but to make sure I hadn't forgotten anything this time round.

# Chapter Seven

...

# Chapter Eight

I could've tried to sell my family home, but I figured there was no use. After what had happened there, no one in the town would want it and anyone from outside of Gundichley would only need to do a quick Google search to see, plus I reckon legally they'd need to be told about it before buying, right? Anyway, it wasn't like I needed the money. Plus it meant I could retreat and fall back to Gundichley if I really needed to.

# Chapter Nine

First I walked by the river searching for a frog. It didn't take too long to find one. They frequented the area, and after a childhood of catching them; I was an expert. I picked him up and looked into his eyes

"Thank you friend," I whispered to him

I held him to the ground and put a pin in one arm, then the other, then his leg and the other. I tapped where his heart would be with my index finger, before slipping him into Abel's sock and burying him in the dirt. We all deserve the cruelty we receive, even if it's for crimes we haven't yet committed. That was one lesson that my mother drilled into me, and she had been punishing me for something awful. Plus my existence alone was terrible to her.

It's a funny thought, being prematurely punished is probably what drives us to our undoing. But I believe that everything must be justified, because why else would I have experienced such cruelty?

The plan was to walk to Toiser and take a bus from there to West Roimhik.

# Chapter Ten

Abel can't stand my silence during sex, so he usually plays music from his phone. Once he tried opera and I held my breath to the point of passing out. When I woke up; he was gone. Seeing me turn up at work the next day made him go pale, he looked sickly. I think he thought I had died so he done a runner, but we never conversed and I wasn't going to break our norm.

Me? I like screamo music, I guess it's because I'm not allowed to release; I like to hear other people scream and live vicariously through their emotion.

# Chapter Ten

# Chapter Eleven

Toiser was a three hour walk away and then West Roimhik was a two hour bus trip from there, so it was a good safe bit of space away from Gundichley.

I jumped a fence, making a herd of sheep disperse - even they were smart enough to avoid me.

After a bit of walking I found myself in a field of purple sedum, where I decided to take a break.

I lay down in amongst the flowers. Not facing the sky like anyone else would, but with my face in the dirt, where it belonged. Maybe if I stayed there long enough I'd decompose and turn into a flower, my first chance to mean something. 'The girl that left Gundichley to become a flower'. I held my face there, as tightly as possible, it was getting warm and moist from my deep breaths. My face started to swell and I could feel my eyes water. The hay fever was bringing feeling to my face, and that feeling was pain. I lay there and enjoyed it.

When I finally decided to pick myself up it had turned dark. Fine by me; I worked better in the dark. Although I needed to be careful this far out, as people here didn't know to stay away from me.

Shortly before arriving in Toiser, I felt a dip inside my bladder, *oh no*. It was starting to turn light, it had become a new day. I would be in West Roimhik late morning/ early afternoon.

Upon arriving in Toiser; everything was still closed, and likely in towns like this, shops wouldn't open until the afternoon. I went to the bus station toilets to find that my fears had been confirmed, I hadn't bled onto my underwear yet, so caught it at the right time. Problem was, I hadn't packed any pads, the shops were closed and there wasn't a vending machine in the toilets, so I had to improvise and hope I didn't get any heavy flow until after I had arrived in West Roimhik. Grabbing the toilet paper roll I wrapped seven layers of paper around the middle part of my pants, then further decided to add another two for safety. It was that cheap thin sandpaper type, so you know the bus company *really* cared about their customers. My poor flower would be ripped to shreds, which I could bear as long as I didn't bleed through - that would be nightmarish.

# Chapter Twelve

West Roimhik was much bigger than Gundichley, but even at that it was only considered a small town. It had all the big brand shops and chains. There were enough people for me to fly under the radar in the way that not everyone knew each other. It was new and big to me.

One of the stops before the one I intended to get off at stopped in front of a small supermarket, a minimarket would you call it? So, I decided to get off a little early and run in to get some pads. Between the running off the bus, my anxiety about being somewhere unfamiliar, and the overheating from being on my period; I was a sweaty mess. While checking out, I noticed a printout saying they were looking for part-time staff, sellotaped next to each till.

I asked about their vacancy and the old woman who was serving me looked down at the pads, then at my face, obviously judging me before throwing an application on the counter. People in Gundichley would have

NEVER treated me like that. It was great, being treated like anyone else, what a thrill! I couldn't help but smile, which made her more weirded out than she already was. This sweat-drenched woman carrying period pads asking for a job, with an unfamiliar (to me anyway) grin was sure to freak out any person of sane mind.

The good thing was: after the incident, my legal second name was changed and because I was a minor; my first name was never mentioned in the papers either. So filling out this application would never lead them to any information about my family, even knowing where I was from. I filled out the application in the store, after using their toilet to put on a pad, removing the now blood-covered sandpaper.

Afterwards I found my way to the estate agents.

"You're Mouna Graham?!" she asked in disbelief.

I didn't know if it was because I was so young or if it was because it was so unusual for someone to buy property over the phone without viewing it first, but again I was enthralled that people felt alright to show their emotions like this around me.

She gestured for me to sit at her desk. "We just need to sign some documents if that's alright with yourself?" Her tone had changed, to what I assumed was her professional non-surprised speech, in comparison it sounded a bit condescending. She stood up, steadying herself on the table. "I'll be right back with the printouts," she gestured her thumb in a vague direction behind her. A rather fast roar of murmurs erupted from behind the door, eyes peering through blinds to look at me as if I couldn't see them, me being a big spectacle wasn't something new but with the reasoning being different; as was my treatment. Instead of people actively looking away from me I now had people trying their best to get to see me. After having signed my life away and paid what I needed she asked, "Do you know where it is?" I wiggled my phone in response. I'd much rather struggle with a maps app than listen to someone give me directions that I wouldn't remember.

# Chapter Thirteen

While walking down the street, a group of young girls stopped in front of me, searching me head to toe, until their leader spoke,

"Lesbian," she spat as the rest of them giggled.

Usually, something like this would put me on edge, but today I was buzzed from the equal treatment and new start, so instead I messed with them.

I smirked and licked my lips.

"Yeah, any of you young ladies interested?"

The leader backed away and the group quickly left, not taking their eyes off me. Imagine being so bothered by how someone else may identify.

I thought the walk would take around thirty minutes, but it turned out to be one hour and seven minutes. I wasn't mad though; I liked the idea of having a little bit of distance between home and the town. After all: I was still just a small village gal.

The building was an old townhouse found popping its head out of a collection of fields.

I put my key in the front door that floated open without any twisting. Maybe one of my new neighbours had left it unlocked, it was the middle of nowhere; anyone that wanted to break in wouldn't travel so far out without tools that'd get them in either way. The communal area was filled with old crusty leaves and a rusty disused bike chained up against the stairway. Two doors on the ground floor for flats one and two, so I made my way upstairs. The wooden steps squealed at each step, edges splintering and crumbling.

My door wasn't so easy as the front. I felt it unlock with my key, but the door didn't seem to agree. I had to barge my shoulder into it, only for it to fly open and create a handle-sized hole in my wall - great start.

Inside, was a bedroom big enough to fit a double bed wall to wall. A bathroom so small that the toilet sat inside the shower and a kitchen that consisted of one counter, two hobs and an oven that wouldn't fit any trays I'd ever seen. There were two cupboards for utensils, one next to the oven and one raised on the wall, both with doors that fell off as soon as you opened them, plus a minuscule fridge built into a cupboard door at the end. The walls were a pasty vomit-coloured green, that I suspect weren't green to begin with. It'd do.

I tested the water, electric and kitchen amenities and it all worked, and that's all I needed. I sat up on the counter next to the hobs and examined my new space. I figured that I needed furniture. So I got on my phone and browsed on the IKEA website, trying to look at what was most popular; what normal people decorated their homes with. Glass coffee tables seemed to sell well, but I didn't care if that was the norm; to me glass tables were for bored housewives seeking mundane thrills wondering if today would be the day they accidentally put their mug down too hard, making the glass fall through.

It took me far too long to determine what I should get. Eventually, I selected a couch (teal, my favourite colour), a wooden dining table and a cheap bed.

I got to the checkout and filled out my details and address, only for it to say it didn't deliver to my address, after all the work I'd put in; I could've thrown my phone across the room.

I sighed and opened up Amazon instead, this time purchasing the first items that came up on my search. I had already curated the right furniture, I wasn't going to spend my time doing it again. I even added a coffee table to this one, again both tables were wooden; because I may be crazy but I'm not stupidly boring and distasteful.

Not only did they deliver to my new home: but they also had next day delivery.

By the time I had placed my order it had gone dark. So I lay down on the counter, my butt dipping into the sink basin and my heels just tapping the hobs, preparing myself for sleep.

# Chapter Fourteen

Waking up to something cold and vaguely wet against my nose, I slowly opened my eyes and I could see something on my face, only a shadow through my bleary morning vision

"Whoa!" I spiked up. A blur of orange flew across the room in a panic. I sat up on the counter, swinging my legs around to dangle over the side. Gripping my hands on the edge of the counter I sighed, dreading following the route of the blur to only find out it was something I had imagined.

I kicked myself off the counter, the floor giving out a wail upon my landing.

I made my way to the bathroom slowly peering my head through the doorway, and there he was, frozen in his tracks staring at me, wondering if he should continue on towards the window. If I had waited just a few seconds longer I would've missed him and be left feeling that I had imagined his presence. A handsome ginger cat. After he realised that

I didn't know what to do; he continued on with his exit. I let out my breath; which I didn't even realise I had been holding.

I checked my emails to find that my delivery was due late afternoon, so I had time to kill.

I looked out the bathroom window, to see where he had gone, and how he was perfectly fine with jumping out a second-floor window. How did he even get in? I caught the back of him dashing into some woodland. A random collection of trees in-between fields with a clear pathway between: manmade. It was unlikely that I'd see the cat down there: so I decided to go on a wander.

Fresh air was replaced by a mix of the smell of manure and woodland. Although there was a clear walkway separating the sections of tree; I could easily lose my mind in thought here. Looking up at the blue skies only burdened by two clouds at most, it was a peaceful day, and I guess a good start to my new life. My phone buzzed. Surprisingly, considering where I was; my phone had perfect service. Without hesitation, I sat on the ground where I was and answered.

"Hello, is this Mouna Graham?"

I crossed my legs into a basket and from nowhere the ginger cat ran toward me. "Yeah." I ducked my head to look at him, putting my hand out to see if he wanted a scratch.

"You applied for a position at our store?"

Luckily I had only applied at the one place, so I knew where he was talking about, but it was so strange that he didn't just say the name of the workplace. The cat brushed his face along the side of my fingers.

"Are you still looking for employment?"

"Mhmm." I'd only applied yesterday; who would get a job that quickly?

"Would you like to come in for your first day tomorrow? 9am?"

I thought in places like this you were supposed to get interviewed before getting a job? Guess not. I got the job at the factory because they accepted anyone that was willing to do the job (which wasn't many people) and they weren't exactly allowed to deny me just because of my family history, whereas other places could use excuses like lack of experience or qualifications.

"Okay." I matched his enthusiasm, which was lacking, and he hung up.

Now I had a new place in a new town, a new job, and a ginger cat friend now curled up in my lap in the middle of this woodland. When I went to put my phone in my pocket he jumped up and ran away. I guess that was the end of our interaction for today. I got up and continued my venture.

I reached what seemed to be the end of the woodland and was faced by a townhouse almost identical to mine. I might've thought I had taken a wrong turn and ended up back home if it weren't for the fact that this building was put together and not worn down like mine. It was almost as if I had stepped into a parallel universe or back in time to see the place in its former glory.

A young boy zoomed out in front of me, then stopped to stare. I awkwardly waved at him, and he beamed a big smile, waving back, then ran to sit on the back stairs of the building, gesturing me over with his hand. He rustled open a packet of crisps and the kid, sitting on the steps, offered me one. I took one and sat on the wall that ran along the side of the steps. I looked at my bear-shaped snack, the empty holes that stood as eyes. I bit off one ear with my front teeth and swallowed it whole, it was so small that I didn't even feel it going down my throat. I did the same with the other ear, then the arms, then the legs. It pretty much melted in my mouth. I looked back down at the kid, to find he had been gazing at me, watching my strange eating ritual, handing me another as if in a trance, wanting me to do it again.

# Chapter Fifteen

It took me until walking back home to realise all I had consumed today was two bear-shaped potato snacks.

Arriving home, I dug through the cupboards, maybe the last tenants had left something? I hadn't even felt hungry until I thought about it, and my stomach panged. My search found nothing, which was probably for the best: this place had been abandoned long enough that the thought of food being here should fill someone with dread. I could've downloaded one of those city apps and ordered food, but in the end I decided to deal with it. My hunger usually passed anyway. I'd buy food after work tomorrow.

My search for food seemed to pass enough time for the delivery to come. Huge thuds rattled the whole building from the front door, forcing me to sprint down the stairs so as not to miss it. Swinging the front door, I caught a high-vis mid walking away.

"You're wearing that?" He raised an eyebrow in judgement. "It's sweltering."

I was wearing my favourite teal jumper with a white shirt buttoned all the way to the top with the collar hanging over the edges of the jumper. Teal is basically the only colour in my small collection of clothing. I guess it's not many people's favourite colour, but teal brings me some sort of comfort, plus I think it suits me. He looked funny with his bright red face, high-vis vest and sweat tickling his forehead, I didn't know how he could've thought to be commenting on my appearance. I understood that it was warm out, but I wasn't a sweaty mess like him.

I led him and his colleague up the stairs to my door while they carried the couch together, they dropped it as I was opening the door and went to collect the other things, again leaving them outside. He dusted his hands together, "Right," he looked at his partner and they headed back to their van. They had just dumped everything outside my door. I didn't exactly want a man's help; but carrying the sofa seemed a two person job.

I got to it, dragging the coffee table in first, then the couch. The couch made scratches on the floor which briefly stressed me out until I remembered that I own the place, and it took me stopping three times before it reached its intended destination. It was only a three-seater but it was heavy. The dining table and bed frame were both flat packed. I carried the mattress and placed it against the cupboards in the kitchen.

I opened up the bed frame flat pack and lay out the pieces in the bedroom to make sure it'd fit. With it being from Amazon I forgot the possibility that it may not have a key. On the instructions there was a picture of a drill. I sighed. Kicking the wooden pieces out of the room, I unwrapped the mattress and lay it on the floor. At least I had something more comfortable to lie on. I'd see if my work sold drills tomorrow, maybe I'd even get staff discount. Walking out the room my eyesight was slowly covered in black followed by the sound of a thud.

Waking up, I felt something weighted on my back, I reached around: touching the fuzz, making me jump a little, before realising it was just the cat. He jumped up and hopped off my back onto the floor.

It was dark out again, I guess I had fainted. When I checked the time it wasn't that late in the evening. I moved to the mattress and set an alarm for the next day.

# Chapter Sixteen

The girl training me was young, probably not long out of school. She wore her hair in a top knot which sat like a fan on her head. She finished most of her sentences in a tone that implied it was a question. After serving my first customer I said, "Thank you, have a nice day." I was shaking, not only had I spoke to the boss but also Daisy *and* the customer. My voice was jittery. It was almost as if I was learning to communicate for the first time and technically - in my adult life - it was. The customer narrowed his eyes and sighed at me before darting away

"What a rude dick," Daisy said loudly, the next customer looked up at her in shock before quickly avoiding eye contact.

After serving my customers with Daisy standing over me loudly chewing gum, I had to ask, "Why the badge?" She didn't understand, so I rephrased it, "Why is it a different name?" Her badge said Lucy, but she had been introduced to me as Daisy.

"Oh, that's because I'm hot." She didn't elaborate on this, and I had no idea what it meant.

The rest of the shift went alright, generally customers were much like that first man, so I quickly learned that less is more with the customer service.

On my lunch break (when I eventually got to eating, even though my hunger had been and gone) one of my colleagues sat across from me.

"New girl, huh?" As he was sitting down Daisy approached and flicked his shoulder with her finger, "Get away, you're not harassing the new starts." The guy shook his hair, and made the effort to wink at me before getting up. She pushed him away from the table,

"So-" she shoved an apple in her mouth and sat down, only to take it back out again without having taken a bite, "where did you move from?" I hesitated while she crunched, and before I could decide if I should be honest or not; she spoke with her mouth full, "Actually, don't tell anyone; it adds to your mysterious vibe, will make it much easier for you to pull too." I didn't know what it was: but there was something I appreciated about her, maybe it was her ability to fill my silences like they weren't of note. She could even turn out to be somewhat of a friend, and with that I was left feeling bold so I asked again about the name tag. She explained that she was young and that there were a lot of creeps in the area, so if they didn't know her name they couldn't stalk her properly.

After my shift, I shopped, gathering everything I needed for my flat.

"Screwdriver, eh?" the guy from lunch approached.

"Yeah, furniture." I was blunt, scanning the shelves and paying him little attention.

"Well, if you need help putting it all together, let me know."

"No thanks-" I squinted at his badge, "Ciaran."

"Ah well, if you need a strong handsome man to help, you know where to find me," he flexed his arms, what a dickhead.

# Chapter Seventeen

After a week of working and living in West Roimhik, I was invited to the monthly work night in a pub.

I exited the toilet stall to find two women making out, one pressed against a sink with her leg being held up by the other. They were fully going into it, but it was still tender, I could only imagine how soft their skin felt touching each other. I could see them manoeuvring their mouths into different positions. They were definitely using some tongue, maybe showing off what skills they could use if they took it further, trying to impress each other, make the hard sell. The blonde one opened up an eye and noticed me.

"Oh," her eyes widened, slowly moving her mouth away from the other woman's and I noticed it was Daisy. "Hey, this is Moon." *Moon*, a nickname?

"Moon, the new co-worker?" The other woman threw a lazy wave. "So..." she glanced at Daisy then at me, "were you enjoying the show?"

Daisy nudged her. "Do you like women, Moon?" She turned her body to face me, her tone sweet, still leaning her side on the sink with the other woman's arm behind her.

"I'm not sure."

"Have you ever kissed a woman before?" the brunette one chimed in, and I shook my head. "Well, which one of us do you find attractive?"

I glanced between them, then looked at them through the mirror on the wall. "You're both beautiful, but I don't think I've been attracted to anyone." I braced for them to treat me like I was a freak, but instead they both shrugged.

"That won't work then, kissing anyone you're not attracted to won't help confirm your sexuality," Daisy stated.

"Maybe she's ace," the other shrugged. Asexual; I suppose that fitted how I felt, although I'd never really been concerned enough to think far into it.

They looked at each other, deep in the eyes and it was as if I had melted out of the room, so I left so they could continue where they left off.

I returned to the table, sitting next to Ciaran.

"Drink?" He offered to buy me another, but I waved my hand down.

The two girls returned from the bathroom, announcing that they were leaving.

"Do you need us to show you where to get a taxi?" Daisy addressed me and I shook my head no. She squeezed my shoulder and they left.

"They're not together you know," Ciaran piped up after some silence. "They have some sort of agreement that if they see each other on a night out and don't pull; they'll go home with each other." I stared at his drink, not sure why he was telling me Daisy's personal information. "Thing is," he continued, "they can pull, quite easily actually, but they always reject the girls because they like each other more, not that they'd admit it," he rolled his eyes before shooting out of his seat and heading to the bathroom. I looked around at our co-workers, sitting in silence staring into their drinks and realised how painfully boring they were without Daisy around. I got up and left, without announcing my departure.

I made it a little up the street before Ciaran appeared beside me, still fidgeting his jacket on.

"I'll walk you home." I waved my hand at him, shaking my head no. "I'll walk you home," he insisted.

We walked in silence until we reached the outskirts of the town.

"You live far out, huh?" I don't know if he was complaining or just wanted to point out the obvious. From the corner of my eye, at the edge of the town I could see a shadow, it was the first time I'd seen one since leaving Gundichley, and almost immediately afterwards I couldn't shake the feeling that we were being followed, although, I was just being paranoid, or so I told myself.

When we arrived at mine he stood eagerly behind me as I opened the front entranceway, trying to slide in behind me.

"Thanks for the walk home, bye!" I tried to cut him off.

"Can I piss?" I pulled my lips to the side. "Come *on*, it was a long walk!" I held the door ajar for him to follow me upstairs, letting him into my flat.

I sat on the couch, naively hoping he'd leave after his 'piss'. I heard the start/stop/start/stop of his choppy pee, I heard the toilet flush, I did not hear him washing his hands. He came out and sat next to me.

"So you were in the toilet the same time as them? Were they making out?" He had his whole body turned toward me, eagerly awaiting my answer.

"Isn't that between them?"

He shook his head. "If you were there, it's between them and you," he said adamantly, "*fuck*." He leaned his head back. Had I chosen to tell him that they even offered to kiss me too; I have no doubt he would've come on the spot. He fixed his gaze back on me, closing his eyes, leaning in and pursing his lips so ridiculously. I didn't move and for a moment I flashed back to being with Abel, until I realised this wasn't Abel, and that I was somewhere new, where I was allowed to react to things. I pulled away.

"Let's have sex," he said, placing his hand on my waist. I shook my head. "Come on!" He pulled on me.

"No." I was firm but he continued to beg and plead. "You realise that you're not taking no for an answer?"

"*SHUT THE FUCK UP!* You bitch! Imagine playing the rape card! I've been nothing but good to you, and what do I get? *This*?!"

Ah yes; be good to someone and they shall need to repay you in sex, I forgot about that law.

"I'm a nice guy, you could never accuse me of that!" He jumped up, grabbing his jacket, "You're a fucking psychopath!"

"Yeah, I know."

He squinted his eyes before darting out of the room. Disaster avoided I guess.

# Chapter Eighteen

I never really liked sex, but I did it with Abel anyway. It's not like I felt anything good or bad from it, it was just: meh. I wish I could feel what everyone else was talking about, to understand why they turn into such hungry animals when sex is on the table, but the idea nor the act have ever given me the thrill that everyone else seems to feel. With Abel at least it was something to do, an opportunity to be close to someone in some way. But being here in West Roimhik I had the option to pass it up, because maybe, just maybe, I'd make a friend and I could be close with them emotionally, and that'd be enough. I didn't have my past holding people back from being around me here, I had the opportunity to have a somewhat (on the surface) 'normal' life.

# Chapter Nineteen

The next day, Daisy arrived late for work.

"Good night?" I asked and she raised her eyebrows.

"Does it bother you that I'm a lesbian, Moon?" she asked while engrossed in stocking a shelf and pretending she'd been here the whole time.

"No, I've never met a lesbian before."

She sniffed in a laughy way. "You're interesting, Moon," she flicked my arm, "enjoy the rest of your night?"

"I left after you, I got bored." I opened another box to unpack. "Ciaran walked me home."

"Well that's uncharacteristically nice of him," she paused for a moment.

"He wanted sex, but I kicked him out."

"That's more like it; what a dickhead."

"That's what I thought."

She laughed, putting her hand on my shoulder, steadying herself at the lower shelves beside me. "Good on you for chasing him away," she mimicked a boxers fighting pose, "I'll tell him off too if you'd like?" I shook my head, she continued looking at the stock while talking, "We're not together by the way," I glanced at her, but her eyes didn't threaten to budge, "me and Roads."

"Roads?" Why would someone be named that?

"From last night; Roads." I scrunched up my face. "*Oooh R-H-O-D-E-S.*" I nodded my head, clearly that was supposed to be better, but it was still a strange name.

"Do you want to be?" I thought Ciaran was right, that they wanted more but were too stupid to do anything, well, not stupid; Daisy was my friend - my first friend - but she was clueless in this instance nonetheless.

She sighed and shook her head, finishing the conversation, even though she had clearly wanted to talk about it.

# Chapter Twenty

There was a knock on my door, not at the front communal area, but my door directly. Opening up to Ciaran was not what I expected from my day off. He was holding two bottles of vodka at either side of his face and pouting. "Hey, I'm sorry about the other night." He pushed past into my home, guess I had a guest now. Taking a seat on the couch, he waved the bottles at me, as if to demand glasses, which I went to get. There was a scratching at my front door, I ignored it and it stopped. Then it started, stopped, started, stopped, started - all while Ciaran was half filling the glasses with unmixed vodka. I finally shot up to check on the noise, catching a glimpse of eyes in a dark corner of the open bathroom - I ignored it. I had never seen the shadows indoors before, this was new. Opening the front door letting in a ginger flash, I didn't know why he was scratching to get in when he'd somehow managed to let himself in otherwise until this point. Sitting back next to Ciaran, he flipped his head over the side of the couch to look into the kitchen, and I took the chance to switch our drinks over - just in case.

"Was that a cat?" I nodded. "I didn't know you had a cat."

"I don't."

He shrugged and raised his glass which was formally mine, moving his head dramatically so that his eyes met mine for the clinking of our glasses, not creepy at all.

A few glasses and I was gone, memories of lifting up the glass and putting it down played in a blurry loop. Waking up on the couch to a note that said *find me outside*.

Things suddenly felt unsafe, and I knew I couldn't stay, because he would just return into my home, so I headed outside.

I stumbled through into the blinded trees, hoping I could at least find my way to that kid's home, towards some sort of civilisation, but my world warped, everything blended together - a world deformed. Was he so dumb that he spiked both drinks? Or did he figure that I'd swap them? He didn't strike me as smart but usually these kinds of people - the type that would spike a woman to gain 'sex' - usually set out with a plan; because they know they're doing wrong. Or was I just really drunk?

So instead of finding other people; I was met by a tree. A tree. Not just any tree. This tree had arms, waving them around like an octopus in water. It belched strange grunting noises toward me, and I wondered if it was trying to speak. Curiously - but still at a safe distance - I walked around it, maybe there'd be a face on the other side and we could communicate better face-to-face. Coming round the edge, I saw a foot, further connected to a leg, I edged further back while still moving around, eager to solve this alcohol fuelled mystery. Next I caught sight of a nude moon, a bare arse. The grunting wasn't coming from a talking tree (what sane person would've guessed?) but instead from a naked man, who I now had a full back view of. He was standing thrusting himself back and forth into the tree, and when I say into: I mean *into.* Shoving his penis into a hole in the tree, having sex with a fucking tree, fucking a fucking tree. I was so entranced watching this that I nearly failed to notice that the loverboy was Ciaran, the same way that he had failed to notice my existence, he was a little preoccupied. I saw his eyes slide towards me without interrupting his stride, my whole head shot down, desperately avoiding his gaze. I blinked slowly, loudly. When I opened my eyes again I was looking in the mirror in my bathroom. In the mirror all I could see was a cruel woman – I look like my mother. A dark shadow stood over my shoulder. I looked to the side and Ciaran was sitting in the bath, his head rolled over to look at me, but his eyes were lifeless and refused to blink. I looked into the bath, he was still naked and covered in bark, it brought a new meaning to 'bark for me'. I examined closer, now standing over him feet on each edge of the bath. His dick had so many splinters in it - I guess 'love' really was painful. I imagined sucking them out - but that's disgusting, plus I didn't want to do anything with him, at least he got laid like he had wanted, even if it wasn't how he had planned, having been with a tree and all. I stumbled off of my perch, I'd let him sleep in my bath, then he could leave in the morning, we were both far too gone for anything else anyway.

# Chapter Twenty-One

I couldn't even bear seeing if he was still in the bathroom. I didn't know how I'd manage working with him now that I'd watched him shag a tree.

I got up and went straight for a walk. The cat joined me through the trees for a while, he kept meowing at me even though I had stopped multiple times to give him a scratch, even cutting across me, nearly tripping me each time. I got bored of it. I picked him up and placed him behind me. He did it again, this time I picked him up and threw him behind me. He still didn't get the hint.

"Ugh fuck off!" I yelled, making his ears go back before scampering away.

I found myself reaching the other house again, the parallel reality. The kid came running towards me from the steps, stopping at my toes, reaching his head right back so he could look up at my face. Why was this kid always outside?

"PAX!!" A female voice screamed in fear from inside, followed by a tall woman wearing a cream knitted jumper and an ugly floral dark green long skirt running out of the building, pulling the kid's arm so hard that I heard a pop. Staring at me, she then crouched down to the kid, waving her index finger at him, "Don't you dare talk to strangers!" 'Talk to' probably wasn't the term she was looking for. "What on earth are you doing?!" She slapped him across the face. *She slapped him across the face.* I felt my face fill with heat and a chill bolted throughout my body. I marched over to her and she stood over me so that I could feel the air spilling from her nose onto my face.

# Chapter Twenty-Two

I woke up on a couch. The kid - Pax - was cuddled up, head on my legs, snoring as a TV flashed in front of us. I gently slid from underneath him, slowly resting his head onto a pillow instead, so as not to wake him. This must've been the other house. I made my way into the bathroom, noticing that my clothing had been changed, and that it had turned to dark outside. I looked at myself in the mirror, seeing a large scratch down the side of my face. I lifted my hand to prod it, and pieces of my arm started to throb as well. I rolled up my sleeves to find I was covered in the same kind of scratches, from what I could only have sworn as a fingernail, however; I didn't remember anything since getting angry at the woman, for hitting a fucking kid.

My hands trembled. This was freaky. Any more freaky than seeing shadow people? Or seeing a guy having sex with a tree that he likely thought was me? Probably not more than; but still strange nonetheless.

I slipped out as quietly as I could, finding that I was running back home, even though I felt like I was floating. Shadows, eyes and trees all blurred together as I hurried my way back to my lightless home. Why wasn't there an outside light anyway?

The front door was wide open and I now approached the stairway at a normal walking pace. I heard one of the other flat doors slam.

"What are you doing here?" I looked to see an older man staring at me, holding a shovel.

"I live here." I gestured up the stairs.

He shook his head. "Get..." he took a deep breath in, "...out of my house!" Before I could respond, the shovel flew toward my face.

# Chapter Twenty-Three

I heard two bangs, those were what woke me up, so I almost wasn't sure if it was part of my dream or part of reality. I looked in everyone's rooms and no one was to be found. It was when I walked down the stairs; that's when I saw it. Blood spread across the walls and my baby brothers lying lifeless with holes in their chests, their insides spilling out. A huge stroke of blood led me into the kitchen, where I witnessed my mother crouched, holding the hand of my father who was quivering and pouring blood everywhere, the edges of my mother's dress dip-dyed in blood that belonged to him. She was holding a shotgun in her other hand. Her head shot up in a demonic fashion and her smile faded into anger as she noticed my presence. "Why couldn't you have stayed in bed?!" I edged away from her. "You always have to ruin everything!" My back hit the wall as she crouched to be face-to-face with me.

I was shaking, I thought I'd meet the same fate as my brothers and father. She caught me glancing at them. "Oh, you really don't think you'd join them, right?" She chuckled at me. "No, no, you don't deserve release, only my lovely *worthy* family," she turned and blew a kiss toward my Father who had just about faded away. "No, you have to stay and suffer." She put the gun to her chin, and in a flash her head was gone, I was blinded by blood in my eyes and shell-shocked by the sound of the bullet. I remember falling, then I remember waking up in the police station.

To my mother, death was a gift; it was something you had to earn through being loved and sweet, two things that I wasn't. Death was a gift and she had deemed me unworthy.

# Chapter Twenty-Four

I woke up and saw him. Standing over me with a worried expression, which quickly turned hard again once he realised I was conscious. This dude really attacked me for no reason *and* neglected to phone an ambulance or even apologise. I started to burn up. My brain fuzzed and refocused red onto him, I was filled with what used to have been blind rage; however now I was conscious to it. I ran into him and tackled him to the ground like a rugby player, on top of him punching, punching, punching, his face splattering into reds and purples. He could easily knock me off him or knock me out again, but my fists wouldn't give his head room to think. Instead my brain ran wild, filling with once forgotten memories of blackouts I'd had since the incident.

I stopped, with him whimpering underneath me, blood sliding off my knuckles, bringing back more memory.

\*\*\*\*

I remember being woken up by a thud, leaving my bedroom to find Ciaran pushing himself back up from the floor. Blood was gliding from his head in the same way it just was from my knuckles. His lower - *torso* - covered with bark. His penis seemingly up and ready for another round. He smiled at me, growling like a dog (why do men think this is attractive?) approaching me.

"Get away Ciaran." He shook his head and continued, I pushed him back, making him stumble. He easily straightened up again, making eye contact. I pushed him again, making him fall into the bathroom, sliding on my bathmat, falling into the bath as his neck made a crunching sound while hitting the wall, his body falling onto the toilet seat. I cocked my head at him, even with his whimpering and whispering pleas; he still didn't seem as desperate as he did when he wanted to sleep with me, the same look in his eyes as Abel had in his the day I left. I remember not even reacting. Stepping to instead look into the mirror, the moment where I woke up from the blackout. I remember standing over him, then going back to bed, if I needed the toilet through the night I'd have to hold it in until he left. However my actions didn't stop there - only my consciousness. Instantly getting back up again and finding that he had stopped whimpering, because he had stopped breathing, so then I began dragging his body, thudding it down the stairs, how the old man didn't hear is a mystery. Clumsily slipping him into a wheelbarrow outside, and following as the cat led me on a journey of twists and turns in the pitch-black, to a spot I'd never find on my own. Sticking pins into his body and burying him. It was so dark on that night that not even I could find the burial site again, which I suppose is great deniability. And it's not like the cat will be able to tell anyone unless he were to manage - with great effort - to find someone else deluded enough to follow him into woods toward the smell of decomposing flesh.

Then I remember getting so angry at Pax's mum that I punched her, full force. She fell, hitting her head off the wall that ran alongside the steps. She started to pick herself back up, but I thrust my hand among her hair and start slamming her head into the brick. She clawed her hands behind herself, digging into my arms, hands, face - anything she could reach - but it couldn't stop me. That time I only lazily dragged the body behind a tree, and felt more concerned with looking after the kid.

And now, having blacked out again remembering all I had done: I sat on top of a dead, limp old man, having beaten him to death, a shadow curling around my shoulder like a hand of comfort, the shadows had always seen me. My throat burned. I hadn't realised at the time but it seemed I had been screaming while burying my fists into him. Not screaming in a way of fear, but more screaming like a triumphant warrior, because that's how I had felt: that I had served myself the tiniest piece of justice.

They all appeared to be accidents, but they were happy accidents, in that I had enjoyed them.

It seemed instead of stopping myself from feeling any emotions like I thought I had; I had been expressing them all along and not letting myself remember, instead letting myself believe that I hadn't been and suppressing it all.

It was undeniable that I would end up getting caught, so there was no point in even hiding the old man. I noticed he had one of those medical wristbands on, I wondered if it was something that could've killed him anyway - when I looked it said dementia, hence his confusion surrounding my being there. Why do people always jump to negatives when they don't understand something?

Ah well, seeing as I was now conscious to it; I might as well have my fun, see if it was better than it was when I blacked out. It was only a matter of time before I got caught anyway.

Time to go home and visit dearest Abel.

Everyone was scared of me in case I was like my mother, turns out - I am much worse.